The Halloween Play

Grosset & Dunlap

Visit <u>www.strawberryshortcake.com</u> to join the Friendship Club and redeem your Strawberry Shortcake Berry Points for "berry" fun stuff!

GROSSET & DUNLAP
Published by the Penguin Group
Penguin Group (USA) Inc., 375 Hudson Street, New York, New York 10014, U.S.A.
Penguin Group (Canada), 10 Alcorn Avenue, Toronto, Ontario, Canada M4V 3B2
(a division of Pearson Penguin Canada Inc.)
Penguin Books Ltd, 80 Strand, London WC2R 0RL, England
Penguin Ireland, 25 St Stephen's Green, Dublin 2, Ireland
(a division of Penguin Books Ltd)
Penguin Group (Australia), 250 Camberwell Road, Camberwell, Victoria 3124, Australia
(a division of Pearson Australia Group Pty Ltd)
Penguin Books India Pvt Ltd, 11 Community Centre, Panchsheel Park, New Delhi - 110 017, India
Penguin Group (NZ), Cnr Airborne and Rosedale Roads, Albany, Auckland 1310, New Zealand
(a division of Pearson New Zealand Ltd)
Penguin Books (South Africa) (Pty) Ltd, 24 Sturdee Avenue, Rosebank, Johannesburg 2196, South Africa

Penguin Books Ltd, Registered Offices:
80 Strand, London WC2R 0RL, England

Library of Congress Control Number: 2004019160

ISBN 0-448-43910-7   10 9 8 7 6 5 4 3 2 1

The Halloween Play

By Eva Mason

Illustrated by John Huxtable

Grosset & Dunlap

It was almost Halloween, and Strawberry Shortcake couldn't wait! She and her baby sister, Apple Dumplin', skipped through the leaves to Angel Cake's house.

"It was berry nice of Angel to invite everyone over to make costumes!" Strawberry said. "What would you like to be this year? A black cat?"

Apple shook her head.

"A clown?" Strawberry guessed. "A ballerina? A pirate?"

Apple giggled, but she didn't say anything.

"Strawberry! Apple Dumplin'!" Angel Cake cried as she opened the door. "Come in! Everyone else is already here!"

"Here are all my art supplies," Angel Cake said.
"And I brought all of my dress-up clothes!" added Blueberry.
"Wow! How will we decide what to be?" exclaimed Strawberry.
"Ooh, I know!" said Orange when she saw some shimmery fabric.
"I bet I'll look really scary in this green paint," Huck said.
"I think I'll use my latest invention as part of my costume," said Ginger Snap. "Guess what I'll make with this?"

Strawberry couldn't wait to find out. She was having so much fun with her friends, she almost forgot her own costume! "Apple!" she called. "What do you think I should be?" But Apple Dumplin' had toddled across the room, carrying an old red tablecloth with her.

Strawberry found her costume in no time. "Look at me!" she cried. "I'm Princess Strawberry!"

Ginger Snap turned a cardboard box into a silver robot costume with flashing lights. Orange Blossom used the fabric to make a set of sparkly butterfly wings.

"Hip-hip-hooray for Halloween!" Angel Cake cheered as she shook her pom-poms in the air.

"Giddyap!" Blueberry Muffin the Cowgirl called.

Rainbow Sherbet was ready for a trip to sea. "Ahoy there, mateys!"

Huck made the spookiest costume of all . . . Frankenstein!

And what about Apple Dumplin'? She made her costume all by herself! "Apple! Apple!" she said happily.

"Good job, sweetie," Strawberry said. "You look just like a real apple!"

"You know what?" Strawberry Shortcake said. "These are the berry best costumes we've ever made! We should wear them for more than just trick-or-treating!"

"I know what we can do!" exclaimed Blueberry. "Let's put on a Halloween play!"

"Ooh, yes!" said Angel.

"That's a berry good idea!" Rainbow Sherbet agreed.

"But a play doesn't sound very spooky," Huckleberry said. "Let's build a haunted house instead!"

"Yeah!" Ginger and Orange shouted.

"If we do a Halloween play," Rainbow Sherbet said, "we can write parts for everyone!"

Ginger Snap shook her head. "The haunted house will have berry spooky tricks. And we can give tours!"

"I vote haunted house," Orange said. "Right, Huck?" He nodded.

"But Rainbow and Angel and I want to do the play," Blueberry said.

The kids turned to Strawberry. She would have to be the tie-breaker.

"I . . ." Strawberry paused. She didn't want her friends to have a big fight. "I'd love to be in the play—and help build the haunted house."

"Fine," Ginger said. "We're going to build our haunted house. Come on, Huck and Orange."

As they left, Angel Cake called out, "Fine! *We'll* do our play!"

Uh-oh, Strawberry thought. *Everyone seems berry upset! And we were having so much fun . . .*

The next day, Strawberry went to Blueberry Muffin's house to rehearse for the play.

"I want to do a Halloween cheer," Angel said. "That should be the big ending."

"How are you going to do a cheerleading routine on a boat?" Rainbow said.

"Why a boat?" Blueberry asked. "Cowgirls have horses, not boats!"

"There has to be a boat," Rainbow replied with a frown.

"Shouldn't we start building the set?" Strawberry interrupted. She was starting to get nervous. How would they finish the script, memorize their lines, and decorate the scenery in time for Halloween?

"The set!" Angel cried. "We forgot about that."

Strawberry was worried. *There aren't enough kids to perform the play and build the set*, she thought. *If only the rest of our friends were here to help.*

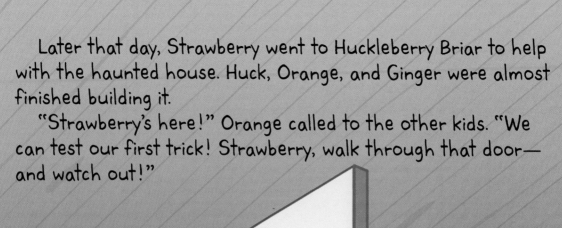

Later that day, Strawberry went to Huckleberry Briar to help with the haunted house. Huck, Orange, and Ginger were almost finished building it.

"Strawberry's here!" Orange called to the other kids. "We can test our first trick! Strawberry, walk through that door—and watch out!"

Strawberry tiptoed through the door. She waited, but nothing happened. "Is that it?" Strawberry asked as she opened her eyes.

Ginger peeked out from her hiding spot. "Did you drop the spider, Huck?"

Huck poked his head out. "I couldn't find it. What about the skeleton?"

"I think it's stuck," Ginger said.

"It's not easy to be in so many places at once," Orange said.

Now Strawberry was worried about the haunted house. *How can we give tours and do the spooky tricks? We really need the rest of our friends!*

When Strawberry got home that night, she was berry tired.
"Halloween is in two days!" she said to Apple Dumplin' and her
pets, Custard and Pupcake. "What if the play never happens and
the haunted house doesn't get finished? What if there's nothing
fun for Halloween—and all our friends are still fighting?"

"I'm sure you'll think of something, Strawberry,"
Custard purred. "You always do."

"If only I could get everyone to work together," Strawberry said. "I just know we could have the haunted house *and* the play."

Apple Dumplin' tugged on Strawberry's shirt. "Pancakes?" she said. "Pancakes for friends?"

"Great idea, Apple!" Strawberry exclaimed. "I'll invite everyone over for breakfast tomorrow and remind them how much fun it is when we all work together!"

The next morning, Huckleberry, Orange, and Ginger were the first to arrive. "You said you had a great idea for the haunted house," Huck said. "What is it, Strawberry?"

Just then Rainbow, Blueberry, and Angel burst in. "What are *they* doing here?" Blueberry Muffin said. "I thought we were going to work on the play!"

"Wait a minute, everybody," Strawberry said. "I've seen the play rehearsals, and I've seen the haunted house. They both need some help."

Her friends nodded, looking down at the ground.

"I thought a lot about this last night," Strawberry continued. "And I know exactly what we need to make this the most spectacular Halloween ever!"

The kids waited. They were ready to hear her out.

"The play needs a stage more than anything," Strawberry said.

"You're right," Rainbow Sherbet said with a sigh.

"And the haunted house needs some people to be tour guides, so the others can do the tricks," Strawberry said.

"We still can't get the skeleton to work," Ginger said.

Strawberry continued. "So if we have the play *inside* the haunted house, it will be one berry big Halloween celebration!"

Nobody spoke for a moment. Then Angel Cake let out a cheer. "Yay, Strawberry! That's a great idea!"

"It's perfect!" Orange said.

"Yeah! Let's get started right now!" exclaimed Huck. "I mean, right after we eat these great pancakes!"

Strawberry grinned at her friends as they sat down to breakfast. *Everyone is so excited!* she thought. *I'm so glad everyone wants to work together again!*

After breakfast, the kids hurried over to
Huckleberry Briar to finish the haunted house.

"The haunted house looks really good," Blueberry Muffin said as she walked around. "How about we hang some spiders up there?"

"We could put a scary ghost over here," added Angel Cake.

"Cool ideas!" Huck said. "Is this a good place for the play? We can add some curtains so it looks like a stage."

"It's just right," said Rainbow Sherbet happily as she hung up some cobwebs around the set.

When the kids had finished decorating the haunted house, Orange Blossom asked, "Can we help with the play now?"

"I'm not sure the play makes sense," Angel Cake said. "What's something a cheerleader, a sailor, a princess, and a cowgirl can all do together?"

"What if they're all best friends?" Ginger asked. "They can have a sleepover at the princess's castle—but it's a *haunted* castle!"

"Ooh, that's berry exciting!" Strawberry exclaimed. "I love it!"

"Me, too!" Angel Cake agreed. "Now let's start practicing!"

On Halloween night, Strawberry Shortcake took Apple Dumplin',
Custard, and Pupcake to the haunted house.

Blueberry and Angel met them at the entrance. "Go-o-o-o-o-od
e-e-e-e-evening," Blueberry Muffin said in a funny voice.

"Woof!" Pupcake barked as a skeleton popped out at them.

"Don't be scared, Apple," Strawberry whispered to her sister. "The
haunted house is just make-believe. I know because I helped build it!"

But when Strawberry Shortcake turned the corner,
a scary Frankenstein jumped out at her!
"Ahhh!" Strawberry yelled. "What a berry spooky
surprise! I wasn't expecting that one."

After the tour, it was time for the play. Strawberry hurried to get backstage for her cue.

"Break a leg, Strawberry!" Ginger mouthed from her seat in the audience—just the right way to wish someone good luck before a play.

Strawberry Shortcake the princess, Rainbow Sherbet the sailor, Blueberry Muffin the cowgirl, and Angel Cake the cheerleader performed an exciting Halloween play. After every scene, the audience burst into applause!

At the end of the play, everyone took a bow.

"I'm so happy we worked together!" Blueberry said.

"Me, too!" Ginger exclaimed.

"Me, three!" Huck called down. He held Apple Dumplin' tight as she played one last trick on her big sister.

"Boo!" cried Apple, giggling as she dangled a spider over Strawberry's head.

"Eeek!" Strawberry shrieked as everyone laughed. It was a berry happy Halloween, after all!